A FIRE
IN THE VILLAGE

A Victorian Adventure

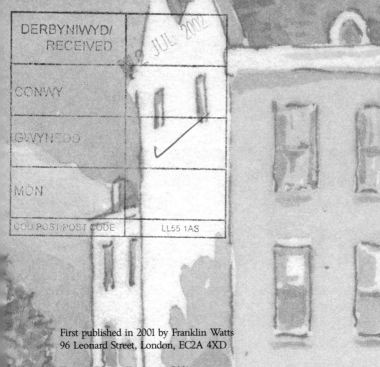

First published in 2001 by Franklin Watts
96 Leonard Street, London, EC2A 4XD

Editor: Louise John
Series designer: Jason Anscomb
Consultant: Dr Anne Millard, BA Hons, Dip Ed, PhD

A CIP catalogue record for this book
is available from the British Library.

ISBN   0 7496 3743 9 (hbk)
          0 7496 4000 6 (pbk)

Dewey Classification 941.081

Printed in Great Britain

THE BIG HOUSE

A FIRE
IN THE VILLAGE

A Victorian Adventure

Written and illustrated by
George Buchanan

W
FRANKLIN WATTS
LONDON•SYDNEY

THE BIG HOUSE

Summer 1858

If you leave the bustling town of Staddon and walk carefully down the track from the common you'll see the small village of Dalcombe, clustered in a steep valley. Stop and look into the distance, where the woods meet the patchwork of fields. You can just glimpse the Big House, Dalcombe Manor.

Mr Edward de Ray lives there with his granddaughter, Charlotte. Charlotte's father Jack, Mr Edward's son, comes to visit them from London from time to time.

Mrs Duff, the cook, lives there too. Her little flat overlooks the orchard. Vincent, the stableboy, occupies a small attic room, and Meg and Mary, the maids, share another.

The houseboys, Albert and Fergus, have the middle room. The window is cracked. I think Fergus broke it – up to mischief as usual!

All the staff are working at the moment. It's a typical day at the Big House...

CONTENTS

CHAPTER ONE
Moving Out

Mary woke up suddenly. Something was clattering on the roof. She could hear what sounded like feet sliding on the tiles and tuneless whistling.

Mary slipped out of bed and walked across to the open window. The maid's bedroom at

Dalcombe Manor was high in the eaves and it offered a magnificent view over the land owned by the master of the Big House, Mr Edward de Ray. This morning the valley was draped in a heavy mist.

Suddenly Mary's view was blocked by a man's head. 'Hurry up with those other ladders!' he shouted.

Then Mary remembered. The roofers! Quickly, she jerked the curtains shut.

'Wake up, Meg,' she whispered, shaking her companion. 'Quick, get dressed, before the workmen see us!'

Meg stretched and opened her eyes.

'It's a shame we've got to move out while they work,' she yawned. 'It'll be strange lodging at Mrs Armitage's cottage.'

'It won't be for long. Mr de Ray said we could have our room back as soon as the roof is fixed. You don't want to stay here and have the rain flooding the place when the winter comes, do you?'

The two maids dressed quickly and hurried down to the kitchen of the Big House.

The kitchen was bustling with people. Mrs Duff, the cook, was handing out mugs of steaming tea to a group of workmen. Members of the Dalcombe Manor staff sat at the big table and Fergus, the houseboy, hurried in carrying a large enamel jug.

'Hot water for Mr de Ray, please, Mrs Duff,' he shouted. 'He wants to get ready quickly this morning, so that he can watch the workmen set up the scaffolding. He's worried about them damaging his flower beds!' Fergus added.

Vincent, the stableboy, stood up when he saw Meg and Mary enter.

'So are you ready then, girls?' he asked cheerfully. 'Mr Portbury is letting me drive you to Mrs Armitage's cottage in his cart.'

'Get away! You'll have us all in a ditch,' grinned Mr Portbury. 'But I did say he could come along. That's if *you* don't mind,' he added, winking at Meg.

'I don't mind at all. He can carry our bags!' said Meg, with a blush.

'Come on,' said Mr Portbury, getting up. 'I'll bring the cart round from the stables. Make sure you're ready and waiting outside with all your luggage.'

It took some time to squeeze the girls, their luggage and Vincent into the cart. The mist had almost cleared by the time they set off trundling into the valley away from Dalcombe Manor.

'Which is Mrs Armitage's cottage, Mr Portbury?' asked Meg.

'It's over there,'
he answered, pointing to a huddle of small
cottages in the distance. 'Are you comfortable,
Vincent? 'Fraid we haven't got room for you up
at the front – too many girls!'

'Comfortable? How can I be comfortable
with these bags in my way?'

Mary laughed, 'Sorry, Vincent.'

'Don't worry, Mary. Vincent can't expect
comfort if he wants to be a coachman like me,'
smiled Mr Portbury.

'And I suppose when I've sat back here long
enough I'll be allowed to grow a moustache just

like yours, too,' joked Vincent. 'Have you noticed his new face furniture, Mary?' he added.

Mary laughed. 'You look very fine with a moustache, Mr Portbury. Mrs Duff was just saying so earlier!'

'Looks more like a scrubbing brush,' muttered Vincent.

'Shut up, Vincent,' Mr Portbury snapped, 'or you'll be walking back to the Big House. You just sit there, keep quiet and learn about driving.'

'Yes, Mr Portbury, Sir,' answered Vincent in a silly voice.

'Less of your cheek, young man!' said Mr Portbury, drawing up ouside a small thatched cottage. 'We're here now.'

CHAPTER TWO
Mrs Armitage's Cottage

An old lady dressed in black was sitting in the shade of her porch, leaning over a cushion perched on her lap.

'That must be Mrs Armitage. Looks like she's making lace. I heard she was the best lace-maker in Dalcombe,' said Mary.

'She still is, I shouldn't wonder,' answered

Mr Portbury. 'Jump down, Vincent. Give the girls a hand.'

'I can't, Sir, my knees have gone all stiff.'

'I said jump!' said Mr Portbury and waved his whip in the air. 'Good day to you, Mrs Armitage,' he said, raising his hat.

Vincent helped Mary and Meg down from the cart and turned back to get their luggage. Mary opened the garden gate and the two girls walked up the path and curtseyed.

'Good morning, Mrs Armitage,' they said together.

The old lady looked up and smiled. 'Good morning, girls. I've been expecting you, Mary and Meg, isn't it? Now, which one is which?' she asked, turning from one girl to the other. 'Mr

Edward told me all about you. The room is ready. It's at the top of the stairs.'

She turned to Vincent. 'Hello, young Vincent! Still being general dogsbody are you? I thought you were going to be a coachman!'

'I am, Ma'am,' Vincent answered, struggling with the bags. 'Just as soon as Mr Portbury gives me a chance!'

'I'm sure you'll do very well,' Mrs Armitage said kindly. 'Just follow me, girls.'

Mary and Meg followed her into the cottage. The room was dark and small, with a rough earth floor and black panelled walls.

A settle stood by the open fire and a table was tucked into the corner by the window, with some stools and a bench.

On the table were six exquisite doilies, made from fine lace.

'Look at this,' said Mary, holding one up to the light and admiring it. 'It's as delicate as a snowflake!'

'Where shall I put these bags then?' asked Vincent, staggering through the door.

'The young ladies are sleeping in the attic room. It's on the left at the top of the stairs,' said Mrs Armitage, indicating a small door by the fireplace. 'I won't go up with you. My poor legs are bad today.'

Meg followed Mary up the winding staircase to the attic. 'This is like my mother's cottage,' she said. 'We're climbing right up by the side of the chimney.'

'Hey! Would one of you take one of these?' Vincent called, struggling up the narrow stairway with the bags. 'I'm getting stuck. These stairs are so narrow!'

'Best thing is to bring the bags one at a time, Vincent,' suggested Mary. 'That'll make a few journeys for you. Hang on Meg, don't push, I'm trying to open the door!'

The latch shot up and Mary threw open the narrow door. They stepped into a long room with wide floorboards. To the right and left, the whitewashed ceiling slanted to the floor. Tucked into the eaves were two mattresses covered with patchwork covers and a table fitted with a china washbasin stood behind the door. The room was tidy and clean.

Mary walked across their new bedroom. The window was so tiny that she had to crouch to look out of it.

'I can see a well,' she reported, 'and a pig sty. And there's the prettiest little shed at the bottom of the garden. It's covered in roses!'

'Who's sleeping where?' interrupted Vincent, panting.

'Put the bags on the bed, handsome!' laughed Meg. 'Either one, it doesn't matter!' she added as Vincent hesitated, looking from one mattress to the other.

Vincent threw the bags on the nearest bed and backed to the door where he stood fingering the latch. 'Right, that's me done. Do you girls want a lift back to the Big House?'

'We need to change into our uniforms first, Vincent,' said Mary.

'Right, hurry up then,' said Vincent and exited down the narrow staircase.

'Come on, Meg. Let's get a move on and try to catch that lift.' Mary opened a case and pulled out her blue housemaid uniform. 'Mrs Duff said there was a lot to do today.'

CHAPTER THREE
Settling In

When Meg and Mary arrived back at
Dalcombe Manor, Mrs Duff was busy peeling
a huge basket of apples.

'What do you think of your new lodgings
then, girls?' she asked as they trooped into the
big, bright kitchen.

'It's just the one room, Mrs Duff,' said Meg.

'It's big, but it's not as nice as our room upstairs here,' added Mary.

'Well, it's a roof over your head!' said Mrs Duff. 'Take a knife and help me with these apples and then you can start on the laundry. Fergus has got the boiler going now so, by the time these apples are ready, the water will be hot enough.'

'He's good, isn't he?' said Meg.

'Who is?' asked Mrs Duff.

'Fergus, the new houseboy.'

'Yes, he's a bright one,' agreed Mrs Duff, 'but he's as much trouble as a bagful of monkeys. If I take my eyes off him for just one minute –'

Mrs Duff broke off and listened. Something was rumbling across the cellar floor. 'Speak of the devil,' she sighed. 'Ask him to light a fire and he spends the next hour playing on the coal trolley.'

She walked quickly to the cellar door, and opened it. 'Fergus Donovan!' she shouted. There was a rustle and some giggling and Fergus appeared at the foot of the steps.

'Come up here!'

Fergus climbed into the room. He was followed by a small, grubby figure.

'Oh, it's you Miss Charlotte. I don't know what your grandfather, Mr Edward, would say if he knew you'd been playing on the coal trolley!' Mrs Duff looked with horror at the black coal smudges on Charlotte's pretty dress.

'Run away to your lessons, or Miss Franks will be looking for you.'

'She already is, Mrs Duff!' chirped Fergus. 'She's searching the loft over the stables, so we came across here to get away. It was a narrow escape!'

'Fergus, you have better things to do than help Charlotte escape from Miss Franks! Go to the laundry and make sure the water is hot. Mary, take Charlotte, clean her up and run her straight to Miss Franks, please.'

'Oh, Mrs Duff, it's French this morning and I hate French!' Charlotte stuck out her lower lip.

'Get away with you, Madam!' said Mrs Duff. 'And Fergus, you run along now.'

Fergus followed Mary and Charlotte out of the kitchen, leaving Meg alone with the cook.

'Mrs Duff, what do you *really* think of Mr Portbury's whiskers?' asked Meg, peeling one of the apples.

'Rats have whiskers, Meg, and mice.'

'Don't forget Mr Jack! He's got a bushy moustache, too.'

'I've already mentioned him,' said Mrs Duff, sourly.

'Which one is he then?' laughed Meg. 'Is he a rat or a mouse?'

Mrs Duff looked round. 'Both vermin, aren't they?' she said. 'How he comes to have such a lovely child like Charlotte, beats me.

'I'll put the pears on to simmer now, Meg. You go over and do the laundry with Mary and, after that, it will be time to walk back to Mrs Armitage's. You'll soon get used to your new room.'

But that first night in the unfamiliar bedroom, the girls found it difficult to sleep. They dragged the two mattresses together for company and chatted quietly.

'Thank goodness Mrs Armitage finally got to bed.'

'Yes, it took her ages to get up those stairs.'

'I like her though, Mary.'

'So do I. She's lovely, isn't she? I think she likes us being here, too.'

'Company, I suppose.'

'While you were washing up, she was talking about how nice it was to be a help. She said when old people like her couldn't help any more, they got sent to the workhouse.'

'What a terrible thought. They're dreadful, cruel places!'

'She said it's her worst fear, to be sent to the workhouse. She got quite upset.'

'It must be sad when you're old. She must be at least eighty. I bet most of her friends are dead now.'

'Well, Mr Edward's still alive. Mrs Duff says Mrs Armitage was Mr Edward's nurse when he was little. Think how long ago that must have been!'

'He's kind to let her stay in this cottage, isn't he? It's a pretty place.'

The girls could hear mice running about in the thatch and the steady patter of raindrops falling on the rooftop.

Mary shrugged off her blanket and went across to close the tiny window. 'It's really pouring down, now,' she said.

For a moment she stood with her hand on the catch, looking out into the dark night. An owl hooted in the back garden. The pig in its low stone sty heard the owl, and grunted in reply.

'I do love pigs,' said Mary. 'I hate it when they have to be killed for food. Mrs Armitage says his name is Samson. Maybe we can go down and feed him tomorrow?'

And firmly closing the window, Mary ran back to her warm bed.

***

The next morning they met Samson. After breakfast, Meg and Mary carried a steaming bucket of mash to his sty and watched with awe as he thrust his eager snout into the trough.

Samson was a king amongst pigs. He was sleek and strong. Mary and Meg both knew a lot about pigs – pigs were winter food.

Samson was ready to be slaughtered soon. He would probably be killed outside in the backyard.

'He'll be slaughtered Saturday week, my dears,' said Mrs Armitage, when they asked her later. 'And we'll have a party! Last year Mr Edward came and Mr Jack with little Charlotte. Mrs Duff always comes – she loves pork, you know. That young Vincent might be allowed, too!'

'I think we'll hide upstairs for the actual killing,' said Meg.

'But we'll come down for the fun!' said Mary.

'Girls, it's a quarter to seven. Aren't you supposed to be on duty in fifteen minutes? Better get a move on!' said Mrs Armitage.

CHAPTER FOUR
A New Invention

It was a long day for the girls at the Big House and it was evening when they left to walk down to the cottage.

They clambered over a stone stile and stood on a low hill looking down into Dalcombe.

Below them they could see the dull glow of a fire and hear the distant clamour of voices.

'Mary!' shouted Meg eagerly, 'that's the Steam Engine. Mr Portbury saw it this morning. He said it was threshing corn right outside Mrs Armitage's cottage. Let's hurry!'

Gathering their skirts they hurried down the hill into the village. An excited crowd was gathered in the lane outside the cottage.

A steam engine stood hissing and juddering in the meadow opposite. It shuddered with life, its black funnel belched smoke and sparks and its huge flywheel flashed round and round.

'What's it doing, Mr Grieves?' Mary tugged at the sleeve of the tall man standing next to her.

'It's a new engine called a portable and it's powering that great threshing machine,' said Mr Grieves, Mrs Armitage's neighbour.

He pointed to a wooden contraption almost as big as the cottage. 'They've been at it all day. See those chaps on the wagon? They're pitching the sheaves into the thresher and out come the stalks and the grain. All those sacks have been done today. It would take a team of men a week to do that by hand!'

'Mind those sparks!' someone shouted. A shower of sparks erupted from the long funnel.

'Watch the thatch, now!'

The girls watched as the sparks curled and dipped in the breeze and gently settled on the cottage roof. Immediately men with long sticks

beat the thatch and extinguished the sparks.

'Where's Mrs Armitage? Is she in the cottage?' Mary asked.

'She's sitting down at the front, enjoying every minute. Never seen anything like it before, I would think,' Mr Grieves answered.

'Let's go and find Mrs Armitage,' said Meg to Mary.

They found her sitting in a low chair. 'Have you come to help me inside?' she asked.

'Give me a hand up. All these new inventions, they'll throw people out of work, you mark my words!' she said.

Mary took her arm, and they walked slowly back towards the cottage. They stopped at Samson's sty, but the pig cowered in a corner and wouldn't let them tickle his bristly ears.

He was either ill or sad and Mary knew which it was: he knew he was going to die.

He had known from the moment on Thursday when Mr Hopkins, the pig sticker, carried the pig bench into the backyard and set it by the sty.

Mary was sure he could smell the blood, even though it was scrubbed almost white. She didn't want to be there when he was killed.

'Mrs Armitage,' asked Mary, 'do I have to be here on Saturday night? I'd rather be at the Big House. Mrs Duff and I could bottle some of those apples Vincent brought and she could teach me how to make honey cakes.'

'Mrs Duff will be down here on Saturday night, dear,' replied Mrs Armitage. 'Along with Mr Edward and Mr Jack and all the staff. You'll have to be here, helping me with the food!'

'What do you do?' Mary was surprised. Surely Mrs Armitage was too old to cook?

'Why, I fry the skin on the fire to make crackling. I've always done that. Cut thin, it's a treat you know – if you've got the teeth for it, that is,' she laughed.

'I'll help inside the house,' decided Mary,

'getting the fire ready and setting the table. Then I'll go upstairs when they kill poor Samson.'

'You do that, my dear. Now I think I'll go to bed. It'll be a big day tomorrow.'

'Do you want help with the stairs?' said Meg.

'Thank you, dear, that would be lovely. I can manage by myself, you know, but it's always nice to have help.'

Meg went first and pulled. Mary went behind and pushed. Mrs Armitage moved painfully. The steps were steep, she was short of breath and her long black skirts got in the way.

'I count the stairs,' she gasped after a while. 'That's seven, six more to go! Nearly there,' she added happily.

CHAPTER FIVE
The Slaughter

Saturday dawned bright and warm, with a gentle breeze. Two large barrels of beer had been rolled out into the backyard and set up on coffin stools, ready for the party.

Meg and Mary cleared out the shed and pulled out a broken ladder, two spade handles and an old table to make a bonfire later on.

Then Mary went next door to see Mr Grieves to collect a couple of long firebrooms.

'You won't need them, Miss, not with the breeze in this direction. All the sparks will blow away from the cottage,' he said.

'I think I'll take them anyway, just in case, Mr Grieves.' Mary took the brooms and leant them against the wall by the back door.

Twice she started up the garden to say farewell to Samson and twice she turned back, tears on her cheeks.

Instead she darted into the shed, seized the hammer and ran round to see Mrs Armitage's other neighbour.

Mr Hopkins was in his backyard, sharpening a long knife. Mary watched as the steel glinted menacingly and a shower of sparks sprayed over his knotted hands. Mr Hopkins stopped and looked up at Mary.

'Can you stun him before you kill him, please, Mr Hopkins?' she said her eyes swimming with tears, as she offered him the hammer.

'Bless you child!' he said. 'That'll be the very first thing I do. He won't know a thing. Now run away and leave me to get on with my work.'

At six o'clock, they lit the bonfire. For a while Mary watched it anxiously, but the wind had risen and the smoke and sparks streamed safely down the garden towards the pigsty.

Mr and Mrs Hopkins arrived with knives, the hammer and a saucepan to catch the blood.

Soon, more people arrived and stood round the fire chatting and laughing. They saw Mr Grieves and Mr Hopkins stride up the garden to fetch Samson. The girls hurried inside.

There was a roaring fire in the grate. Mrs Armitage was sitting on her settle preparing to fry the pig skin and Mr Edward and Jack de Ray were talking to her. They looked up and the girls curtseyed. Mr Jack winked at the girls.

'Fetch me a beer, girls,' he said, 'then I'm going outside to watch the fun.'

Fun? The girls looked at each other. They could hear Samson squealing.

'I'll go and get it,' Mary gulped and rushed out of the back door.

Mr Grieves and two helpers were struggling with Samson. Mr Hopkins was shouting and leaping around with the hammer in one hand and the knife in the other, waiting to strike. Samson was screeching and grunting and howling, fighting for his life. Mary grabbed a tankard of beer, turned and collided with Mr Jack who was coming through the back door.

Beer sluiced over his waistcoat.

'STUPID GIRL!' he yelled.

'Sorry! It was an accident. I didn't mean ...'
Mary gasped and feeling sick and faint rushed
upstairs to the bedroom.

'Fetch me a towel!' shouted Mr Jack, to no
one in particular.

'Here you go, Sir!' called out Fergus running
over holding out a towel.

'Thank you, Fergus,' muttered Mr Jack,
glancing around at the staring faces.

The din in the yard grew louder as the men
continued to try to catch Samson. Inside the
cottage, Mr Edward turned to Meg.

'Go and look after Mary,' he said kindly.
'Mrs Armitage can manage for the moment. I'm
going outside to help.'

'That's right, my dear!' said Mrs Armitage
and patted his arm.

After Mr Edward had gone she leaned over
and tossed more coal onto the fire. Slowly, she
picked up the large frying pan, slid it onto the
grate and lodged it in the flames.

She watched it for a while and the smell of
hot fat reached her nostrils. She sat back on the
settle, closed her eyes and waited for the men to
bring in the strips of skin for her to cook.

Upstairs, Meg hugged Mary. 'And do you know what I saw?' she asked, desperately trying to find something to say that would interest Mary. 'Mrs Armitage called Mr Edward 'dear'! And she patted his arm. Just fancy that!'

'What's happening outside?' Mary cried. 'Is it over yet?'

Four men are holding him to the fire. We'd

better go down in a minute,' replied Meg.

Downstairs Mrs Armitage dozed. The fire licked the edges of the frying pan.

Suddenly, there was a hiss as the hot fat splashed and a great flame shot up the chimney.

The frying pan tipped, there was another roar and this time the soot in the chimney began to burn with a noise like an approaching express train, getting louder and louder every second.

Mrs Armitage woke up with a start.

The girls were upstairs! As quickly as her frail, old body would allow, she opened the door and began to climb the stairs to warn them.

Outside Mr Jack was making a short speech. He stood and raised his tankard to honour Mr Hopkins, the pig sticker.

No one saw the showers of sparks shoot up out of the chimney onto the thatch, followed by the long yellow flames which licked and curled in the night sky.

No one noticed the red hot patch of smouldering thatch, or the wisps of smoke until, with a roar, the whole roof burst into flames.

There was shouting and orders were thrown around. Men frantically beat the thatch with firebrooms, others ran to collect ladders and fill buckets from the well. Mr Grieves and other helpers raced off to alert Mr Norris, the fireman.

CHAPTER SIX
Fire!

'Girls, girls!' called Mrs Armitage from the stairway. 'Come downstairs!' Her feeble voice was drowned out by the roar from the chimney.

She heaved herself up onto the next step and gasped for breath. Smoke was curling through the cracks in the stonework and entering the stairway. It was stifling. At the top of her voice, she shrieked, 'Fire! Fire!'

Upstairs, Mary heard the faint cries. 'Look!' Mary screamed and pointed to the ceiling. It was smoking and cracking and, with a loud crash, a whole section of plaster gave way. A shower of sparks and lumps of burning straw thudded onto the floorboards.

The girls tumbled down the spiral stairs. Behind them beams and thatch crashed down. Smoke filled the narrow stairway. Coughing and spluttering they passed the door to Mrs Armitage's bedroom.

'Hurry up!' screamed Meg. 'Don't stop!'

But Mary had found Mrs Armitage crumpled on the stairs.

Mary looked back at Meg. 'Get help, Meg! Quickly!' she screamed.' Mary knelt and tried to rouse Mrs Armitage.

Meg turned and rushed back up the stairs. She burst into the smoke-filled bedroom, grabbed the window catch and threw the window open.

She gasped the fresh air. 'Help,' she cried feebly to the figures running round outside, just

before falling into a dead faint.

Mr Norris and his firefighters had arrived with the fire engine. They had dragged it down the lane and were reeling out the hoses, filling the water tanks from the well.

'Someone's upstairs! I saw them at the window! Fetch a ladder!' shouted Mr Grieves.

But Mr Norris didn't wait for a ladder.

'Call the doctor,' he shouted and pulling up

his collar, ducked his head and ran inside the burning cottage.

He hurled aside the fallen settle and charged for the stairway.

It was hot, dark and smoky inside. He slowed down and, using his hands to feel the way ahead of him, began to climb the stairs.

The racket was deafening, the fire roared and stones snapped and cracked in the heat. His fingers touched some cloth, a hem, then a foot.

There was a body on the stairs! Struggling, he pulled the dead weight towards him and staggered backwards down the stairs.

Outside, the fire engine was in action. Men heaved and pulled at the long pump handles. Jets of water sluiced onto the thatch.

Mr Grieves raced up the ladder, reached in through the window and pulled Meg's unconscious body over his shoulders.

Gingerly, he clambered down. Hoses jetted water into the bedroom, killing the sparks. A fireman climbed inside, dragging a hose behind him.

Mr Grieves placed Meg carefully on the grass and she lay shivering, wrapped in a blanket.

Suddenly there was a cheer and the men working the pumps looked up to see Mr Norris burst out of the cottage, carrying Mrs Armitage.

Mr Norris laid Mrs Armitage next to Meg on the grass. 'Help her, she's still breathing,' he gasped and staggered back to the blazing cottage.

Two men grabbed him. 'Don't go back in there!' they shouted. 'It's too dangerous.'

'There's someone else!' he yelled. 'Get out of my way!' Thrusting them aside, he covered his face with his arm, strode through the cottage door and approached the black staircase for a second time.

He crawled up the hot stones, searching desperately with his hands. 'It's the other maid, Mary. It must be her,' he muttered to himself, as the smoke enveloped him.

CHAPTER SEVEN
The Workhouse

The crowd outside waited with bated breath for what seemed like an age.

Then, suddenly, a cheer rose as Mr Norris appeared at the upstairs window, holding a limp body in his arms.

He leaned out and handed Mary to a fireman waiting on the ladder and quickly climbed out of the window.

The fireman laid Mary on the grass, next to Meg and Mrs Armitage. Her clothes were charred, her hair was singed and the backs of

her hands were blistered and swollen.

Mrs Duff gently stroked Mary's head. 'She's coming round, Sir,' she said, looking up at Mr Edward de Ray. 'She must have been helping Mrs Armitage. What a brave girl she is, staying to look after her.'

Mr Edward bent over. 'Mrs Duff,' he said, 'can you care for these two courageous girls for the next few days? Keep them comfortable, lavender for the burns, camomile for the blisters. You know what to do, I'm sure, and Dr Brown will always give you advice. As for poor Mrs Armitage...'

He went across to where Mrs Hopkins was cradling Mrs Armitage on the grass. Mrs Armitage was white and shaking and tears were

rolling steadily down her cheeks.

'Oh, Mr Edward, I'm so sorry,' she wailed. 'I must have nodded off. It all happened so fast! How are the girls? What will happen to me?' she sobbed.

Jack de Ray walked over and tapped his father's shoulder. 'Don't worry, I've already taken care of Mrs Armitage, Father,' he whispered into Mr Edward's ear.

Mr Edward shot upright. 'Whatever do you mean?'

'Well, Father,' he began. 'She's got nowhere to go, so I told Vincent to ride into Dalcombe and have a word with Mr Moore at the workhouse. It's best to act quickly in these situations, you know. That's his cart arriving now, I think.'

Mrs Armitage, overhearing the conversation, began to tremble and wail even louder.

Mr Edward swelled with rage. He grabbed Mr Jack by the elbow and pushed him towards the lane, away from Mrs Armitage.

'You wicked boy! Have you no Christian charity?' he roared. 'Go straight over to Mr Moore and apologise for calling him out. Give him a few guineas for his trouble and send him on his way!'

Mr Edward strode back to Mrs Duff. 'They'll come to the Big House with us, Mrs Duff,' he said. 'Hurry back and turn three empty rooms on the first floor into a sick bay for Mrs Armitage, Meg and Mary. Mr Portbury will take you.'

'Which empty rooms, Mr Edward?' asked Mrs Duff, puzzled.

'Jack can be charitable for a change. Clear his things out and put in some extra beds. Mr Portbury!' he shouted, turning to see his coachman backing off into the shadows. 'Mr Portbury, take Mrs Duff back to the Big House, as quick as you can, please.'

Mr Portbury stepped out into the light. Under the shadow of his hat, his face was covered in soot and dirt.

'Whatever happened to you, Mr Portbury?'
Mrs Duff asked, leaning forward to get a better
view. 'Are you all right?'

'Lost half me moustache,' mumbled Mr
Portbury. 'Bit of
burning thatch blew
off the roof, caught
my moustache and
whoosh, up it went.
No good having
half a moustache,'
he rambled on, 'the
whole lot will have
to come off now!'

Mrs Duff
snorted with
laughter and then
quickly turned it
into a cough.

'It's an ill wind,'
started Mr Edward
and then bit his lip. Mr Portbury had been
bravely helping the firemen. It was no time for
jokes. 'Thank you for your help, Mr Portbury,'
he said instead.

CHAPTER EIGHT
A New Home

For three days, Mrs Armitage, Mary and Meg were confined to their beds in the darkened rooms in the sick bay.

On Dr Brown's orders, the long velvet curtains had been kept firmly closed. The rooms were warm and richly furnished, full of beautiful things. Their beds, with down mattresses and soft cotton sheets were blissfully comfortable. Mary and Meg were feeling much better.

'It's like sleeping on clouds,' said Meg and turned to look at Mrs Armitage. She was sobbing again. Meg crept out of bed and leant over her. 'Mrs Armitage,' she said gently, 'whatever's the matter?'

But Mrs Armitage kept her eyes tight shut and said nothing.

'Please tell us, Mrs Armitage. What is it?' asked Mary.

But Mrs Armitage just lay on the bed and sobbed.

'I think she's still frightened of being sent away. She thinks they'll send her to the workhouse when she's better,' whispered Meg. 'She's not even touching her food. We'll have to tell Mrs Duff.'

'But Mrs Duff said Mr Edward was going to let her live in the gatehouse when she's better. You know, that tiny place at the bottom of the drive with the tall chimney,' said Mary.

'Then Mr Edward had better tell her,' said Meg. 'I must speak to him.' She struggled out of bed and reached for a robe.

'I'll come with you,' said Mary, following her friend's example.

The two girls slipped out of the door. The strong sunlight in the hall made them both blink. Meg held tightly onto the stair rail and Mary held even more tightly onto her friends hand. Slowly, they made their way to Mr Edward de Ray's study.

Mr Edward was writing letters at his desk. He looked up at the two girls as they entered.

'Mr de Ray, we're worried about Mrs Armitage. She doesn't seem to want to get better. We think she's frightened that you're still going to send her away,' Meg explained.

'Send her away?

'Yes, to the workhouse.'

Mr Edward stood up. 'Certainly not,' he said. 'I'll speak to her now,' he said sweeping out of the room.

The girls waited a while and then made their way back to the sick bay. What a change greeted them. The heavy curtains had been thrown open and light flooded the room. Mrs Armitage was sitting up in a chair by the window. A bright smile wreathed her wrinkled face.

'Oh, girls,' she smiled, throwing her arms open. 'Mr Edward says I can move into the gatehouse. I'm going to live there for the rest of my life!'

The girls went over to her. Mary took one of her knarled old hands and Meg took the other.

'That's wonderful news,' said Meg. 'And when you've moved in, are you going to show us how to make lace, Mrs Armitage?'

'I'm not waiting until then,' she said. 'Mr Edward said I was to teach you two young girls about lacework. If I leave it much longer, you'll be as old as me!' she cackled.

'Mary, why don't you see if Mrs Duff has some thread and bobbins?' Mrs Armitage added. 'Oh, and you might want to ask her for some honeycakes, too. If I'm going to work, I'll have to eat.'

Mary and Meg smiled at each other and Mary made her way to the door.

'Oh, and Mary?' Mrs Armitage called after her. 'If you see him on your way down, will you say thank you? He always was such a dear boy.'

'Who?' asked Mary, but they both knew who she meant.

'Why, my Edward, of course,' said Mrs Armitage, with a proud smile.

THE BIG HOUSE

NOTES

LACEMAKING

Lacemaking was a skilled cottage craft. Very little equipment was needed - a hard pillow, some wooden or bone bobbins, pins and thread and scraps of parchment.

There were special lacemaking schools which taught the craft, as well as the three R's, to children from the age of four. By the age of seven many children would be able to use their skills to supplement their household's income.

Machines which could imitate lace patterns

were invented in the middle of the 19th century, and the resulting cheap lace drove the cottage industry almost to extinction.

COTTAGE PIGS

Many cottagers kept a
pig, feeding it on
household scraps.

In hard times,
neighbours would
help by contributing
additional scraps of
food. When the pig
was slaughtered,
they would expect
some cuts of flesh
in return.

Pigs were
slaughtered in the
autumn and the flesh
was cured, salted or smoked
for use during the long winter.

STEAM ENGINES

Steam power was introduced into farming in the mid 1850s. At first steam engines were horsedrawn and were known as portables.

By 1857 the first self-propelled traction engines were introduced to plough, draw carts and providing power for all kinds of farm machinery.

Later in the century, some engines were adapted to burn straw. These engines were exported to the plains of America and Russia, where supplies of straw were plentiful and cheap and coal and wood were expensive.

FIRES

Most villages and towns had local fire services which were manned by volunteers.

Sometimes a parish would buy a fire engine or a rich benefactor would buy a machine for the use of the village.

Fire engines were usually horsedrawn, although for short distances the volunteers would drag them. Pumps were powered by hand, usually requiring several men per handle.

THE WORKHOUSE

In the 19th century local parishes were responsible for looking after their own poor.

After 1834, parishes were encouraged to join together to jointly fund a 'union workhouse' to house the poor. This would have been under the control of a manager or a governor.

Conditions were deliberately harsh to discourage the fit and healthy from seeking charity. Families were separated, parents were often refused permission to see their own children, even though they were in the same building, and the healthy were given work.

Stone-breaking, grinding corn and bones by hand and picking oakum were typical occupations, although the grinding of bones was abandoned after it caused a severe outbreak of disease.

The workhouse gained a reputation for being heartless and grim and even though workhouse conditions improved in the 1850s, they never completely lost their harsh and uncaring image.